PONYVILLE MYSTERIES

Cover design by Christina Quintero. Cover illustration by Franco Spagnolo.

Little, Brown and Company
Hachette Book Group
1290 Avenue of the Americas, New York, NY 10104
Visit us at lb-kids.com
mylittlepony.com

First Edition: July 2017

Little, Brown and Company is a division of Hachette Book Group, Inc. The Little, Brown name and logo are trademarks of Hachette Book Group, Inc.

The publisher is not responsible for websites (or their content) that are not owned by the publisher.

Library of Congress Control Number 2017939788

ISBNs: 978-0-316-43168-2 (pbk.), 978-0-316-43169-9 (ebook)

Printed in the United States of America

LSC-C

10 9 8 7 6 5 4 3 2 1

Schoolhouse of Secrets

by Penumbra Quill

Little, Brown and Company

New York Boston

The Pony stared out the window at the quaint cottages spread out below. Ponyville was small. Much smaller than from where The Pony had traveled. The large and tacky castle nearby was clearly a later addition and, in The Pony's opinion, stuck out like a sore hoof. But then, the princesses of Equestria were never known for being subtle.

However, it was the endless forest beginning at the very edge of town that truly held The Pony's attention. This was why The Pony had uprooted everything to move to this backcountry village. The Everfree Forest contained secrets yet to be discovered. Ancient secrets. Dangerous secrets. Secrets that would make the pony who uncovered them very powerful. And now, here The Pony was, living just a few short steps away.

It was time to get started.

CHAPTER ONE

It was another typically perfect morning in Ponyville. The sun shone brightly as ponies, Unicorns, and Pegasi bustled about. They opened their shops, ran early-morning errands, and generally got their days started. Some of the younger members of Ponyville rushed through town toward the Schoolhouse. Apple Bloom, Sweetie Belle, and Scootaloo trotted alongside one another, just like they did every morning. Apple Bloom usually talked nonstop the entire way to school, but not today. Scootaloo smacked her with a wing.

"Spill it!" she ordered.

"What?" Apple Bloom asked.

"You're really quiet this morning,"

Sweetie Belle explained. "You not talking? That's weird."

"It's nothin'!" Apple Bloom said casually. Snips and Snails rushed past them toward the Schoolhouse.

"Mornin', Crusaders!" Snips called. "Hey, Apple Bloom! Sweetie Belle! Tell your sisters they are *awesome!*"

"We *will!*" Sweetie Belle called back. Apple Bloom sighed. Scootaloo and Sweetie Belle glanced at each other.

"Sister stuff," Scootaloo said. Sweetie Belle nodded in agreement. Scootaloo turned to Apple Bloom. "Okay, what's up?"

Apple Bloom stopped walking and turned toward her best friends. "What are we doin' with our lives?" she asked. Sweetie Belle and Scootaloo stared at her.

"Right now we're going to school," Sweetie Belle responded.

"What do you *think* we should be doing?" Scootaloo asked.

Pip hurried past them, awkwardly dragging a schoolbag that was much too big for him. "Cheerio, ponies! Apple Bloom, Sweetie Belle, tell your sisters top-notch job!"

Apple Bloom gritted her teeth.

"This is about Applejack, Rarity, and that Manticore, isn't it?" Sweetie Belle asked. Apple Bloom nodded. A few days ago, Rarity and Applejack were returning from a friendship mission for Princess Twilight Sparkle when the Friendship Express was attacked by a crazed Manticore. *Of course,* the two of them rushed to the rescue, saved a bunch of ponies, figured out what the misunderstanding was, befriended the creature, and saved the day. It was all *any*pony in Ponyville could talk about.

"What? You wish they *didn't* defeat the Manticore?" Sweetie Belle asked.

"Of course not," Apple Bloom said defensively.

"Are you afraid Applejack is gonna like the Manticore more than you? Invite him to live in your room?" Scootaloo asked, grinning.

"No!" Apple Bloom said, laughing.

"Oooh. I bet the Manticore can buck *so many* more apples than you!" Sweetie Belle giggled. "If I were you I'd be really worried!"

"I'm not worried!" Apple Bloom exclaimed. "I'm just wonderin' what's next for the Cutie Mark Crusaders."

"What do you mean?" Scootaloo asked.

"Well, it just seems like there's gotta be something more out there for us to do." It was the first time Apple Bloom had expressed her concern out loud.

"We've been helping other ponies figure out *their* cutie marks," Sweetie Belle answered. "After all, we've had plenty of experience with that!"

"I know, and don't get me wrong. I love that *our* cutie marks are all about helpin' *other* ponies with their cutie marks." The Crusaders examined their cutie marks. Each of them had a matching shield with a different symbol inside. Apple Bloom had a heart inside an apple, Sweetie Belle had a music note inside a star, and Scootaloo had a lightning bolt inside a wing. They were the only ponies they knew in Equestria to have cutie marks that matched this way. "But don't y'all wish it was a bit more . . . exciting sometimes?"

"*Exciting* sounds like another word for *dangerous*," Sweetie Belle admitted.

"You know I'm always up for an adventure," Scootaloo said. "But think about it. We didn't get our cutie marks until *after* we stopped looking for them, right? Maybe some big adventure will pop up when we least expect it to!" Apple Bloom considered that as Diamond Tiara and Silver Spoon came trotting up behind them.

"Morning, Crusaders!" Diamond Tiara called in her singsongy voice. "Did you hear—"

"*Yes!*" Apple Bloom yelled. "*We know all about my sister and Rarity and the Manticore!*" Everypony stared at Apple Bloom, who blushed brightly.

"Sorry 'bout that," she muttered.

"What I was *about* to say before I was *interrupted*," continued Diamond Tiara, "was, 'Did you hear about the family that moved into that old house up on Horseshoe Hill?' There's a *new filly* starting school today and nopony knows *anything* about her except *me*!"

CHAPTER TWO

"My mother heard that her whole family moved here from Trotsylvania," Diamond Tiara explained as they approached the Schoolhouse. She hadn't stopped talking about this new family since she had joined the Crusaders on their walk. "My father says they must be pretty well-off to have bought that house. It's *huge!*"

"I wonder why they moved here," Apple Bloom said. It had been a while since anypony new had come to Ponyville.

"Hey! Maybe we should give the new student a nice, warm welcome!" Sweetie Belle suggested. "Show her how nice it is here in Ponyville?"

"That's a *great* idea!" Scootaloo chimed

in. "And who better to welcome her than the Cutie Mark Crusaders! Right, Apple Bloom?"

Apple Bloom grinned. A Cutie Mark Crusaders welcoming committee might not be the same as saving a train full of ponies from a Manticore, but it would certainly make this new student's day better!

"Sure," she agreed. "Let's go meet this new pony and show her what Ponyville has to offer!" The school bell rang and the ponies hurried toward the Schoolhouse.

"Okay, students! Hurry up!" Miss Cheerilee called from the doorway. "We've got a big day planned!"

Apple Bloom rushed up the stairs behind Scootaloo and Sweetie Belle. There was a buzz of activity as everypony bustled around the room, chatting and joking.

Apple Bloom scanned the room but didn't see anypony aside from the ones she already knew. The hustle and bustle of the room suddenly came to a complete stop. Apple Bloom looked around to see why the students were suddenly so quiet. They were all staring in the direction of the door to the Schoolhouse. Apple Bloom followed their gazes and saw the new student, standing quietly and observing them.

She was a lavender-coated Unicorn. Her bright-blue mane had white streaks in it, as did her tail. Her piercing violet eyes glared out at everypony staring back at her. On her flank was her cutie mark, a spell book under a bright moon with lightning and smoke surrounding it. Diamond Tiara leaned over to Apple Bloom, Sweetie Belle, and Scootaloo.

"I know you all are the experts, but that cutie mark looks pretty ominous to me," she whispered. Apple Bloom didn't disagree, but she knew from experience that not every cutie mark meant what it seemed at first glance. You should never judge a book by its cover. Even if it has a creepy-looking cover.

Apple Bloom glanced at Scootaloo and Sweetie Belle, who seemed a little less excited about being the Ponyville Schoolhouse welcoming committee now that they had gotten a look at the new student. Apple Bloom cleared her throat to get their attention.

"Okay, y'all. Let's say hey!" Apple Bloom trotted over to the new student, trusting her friends to follow. The new student gazed at Apple Bloom, who smiled back and held out her hoof.

"Hey there! Welcome to Ponyville. I'm Apple Bloom. These are my friends, Scootaloo and Sweetie Belle."

"Hi," the new pony said without smiling as she studied the Crusaders. Apple Bloom thought she saw the pony's piercing eyes linger on their matching cutie marks.

"We call ourselves the Cutie Mark Crusaders," Apple Bloom continued, "because...well, that's a long story. But we wanted to welcome you to Ponyville!" Apple Bloom glanced at Sweetie Belle and Scootaloo, nodding at them to introduce themselves.

"Nice to meet you..." Scootaloo paused, waiting for the pony to introduce herself. "Um, do you have a name?"

"Lilymoon," the Unicorn said coolly.

She brushed past the Crusaders and took a seat at a desk, completely ignoring everypony in the room.

"Well," Sweetie Belle said, letting out a big breath. "She's sure friendly."

CHAPTER THREE

The school day passed quickly and
uneventfully. Miss Cheerilee had just as
little success engaging Lilymoon as the
Crusaders did. Aside from repeating her
name and stating that her family was
from Trotsylvania, she remained silent the
whole time.

Pip, Diamond Tiara, and a few others
tried as well, but she would just stare at
them with her piercing eyes and walk away.
Determined to be friendly, Apple Bloom
tried one more time at the end of the day.
She headed over, planning to ask how
Lilymoon's first day went, but the moment
class was dismissed, Lilymoon jumped up
and left quickly. Diamond Tiara and

Silver Spoon joined Apple Bloom on the steps of the Schoolhouse and watched Lilymoon hurry away.

"We're all trying our best to be welcoming," Diamond Tiara huffed, "but if a pony doesn't *want* to be friends with anypony else, far be it from me to force her!" Silver Spoon nodded in agreement and they both trotted off.

"Oh well." Scootaloo shrugged as she hopped down the Schoolhouse stairs. "Guess you can't make friends with everypony. What are we gonna do this afternoon?"

Apple Bloom had an idea. They could go the clubhouse and hang out just like they did yesterday and the day before and the day before. Back when they didn't have their cutie marks, they would spend hours making lists and coming up with schemes. But lately, they just hung out, discussed what had happened at school that day, and then headed home. At least Lilymoon was something new and different. Apple Bloom wondered why a pony would act so standoffish when they were all so obviously trying to make her feel welcome.

"You think maybe she just misses her friends back home?" Apple Bloom asked the others.

"Lilymoon?" Scootaloo laughed. "With an attitude like that, what makes you think she *has* any friends back home?"

"She gave me the creeps," Sweetie Belle added. "The way she stared at us? Spooky."

"Maybe things are different in Trotsylvania," Apple Bloom countered.

"Maybe starin' at ponies is the way they say hello?"

"Why are you trying so hard to defend her?" Scootaloo asked.

Apple Bloom thought for a moment. "I dunno," she answered honestly. "I guess I'm just trying to figure her out."

"Well, just ask her," Sweetie Belle suggested.

"I don't think she's gonna be any more talkative tomorrow," Scootaloo said.

"No," Sweetie Belle said, "I meant ask her right now." She pointed. "Look!"

Apple Bloom and Scootaloo both looked and saw Lilymoon sneaking down a path leading out of Ponyville directly toward the Everfree Forest! The Crusaders hid behind a bush and quietly watched her. Lilymoon peered around to make sure nopony was watching and then carefully stepped over the roots of a large tree into the dark woods.

"Why is she going into the Everfree Forest?" Sweetie Belle whispered.

"Well, there's one way to find out!" Apple Bloom whispered back. "Come on!"

"Why do we even care what the new pony is doing?" Scootaloo groaned.

Apple Bloom didn't answer. She leaped over the roots of the large tree and followed Lilymoon into the Forest. She caught a glimpse of a blue tail with a white streak disappearing behind some trees.

"This way, y'all!" she whispered. The others rushed after Apple Bloom, deeper into the Forest.

They tried their best to follow Lilymoon. But she was quick for a pony who had never explored the Everfree Forest before. After a few minutes, they accepted the fact that she was long gone.

"Why would a new pony go rushing off by herself into the Everfree Forest?" Apple Bloom wondered aloud. "What is she doing out here?"

"What are *we* doing out here?" Sweetie Belle asked, looking around the Forest. "It's gonna be dark soon."

"Yeah, are we done now?" Scootaloo asked.

"Crusaders," Apple Bloom said, turning to the others with a huge grin on her face, "somethin' mysterious is goin' on, and we're gonna find out what!"

CHAPTER FOUR

The next morning, Apple Bloom was determined to get some answers out of Lilymoon.

"We were being 'polite friendly' yesterday," Apple Bloom explained as they headed toward the Schoolhouse, "but today we're gonna get serious about being nice." Sweetie Belle and Scootaloo exchanged looks.

"You sure seem awful concerned about Lilymoon," Scootaloo observed.

"Well, it's like you said," Apple Bloom replied after considering for a second. "Maybe Lilymoon is the thing that came along when we least expected it. Maybe figurin' this out is something only we can do!"

"Do you maybe think you might be overreacting?" Sweetie Belle asked. "All we really know is she's kinda mean and wandered into the Everfree Forest. That's not *that* strange."

"I'm not overreactin'! I just think we should get to know more about her before something strange *does* happen." Apple Bloom walked up the steps of the Schoolhouse and stopped in her tracks.

"Uh. We might be a little late," Scootaloo said.

The inside of the Schoolhouse was an absolute disaster. Somepony had smeared paint all over the walls; stacks of books towered over the ponies, waving precariously back and forth but never quite tipping over; and all the desks and chairs were stuck to the ceiling! It looked like the Crusaders were the last ones to arrive. All the other students were pointing and talking over one another about the state of the classroom. Apple Bloom glanced around quickly, looking for Lilymoon. She saw her over in the corner by herself, observing the mess. Apple Bloom couldn't quite read her expression.

"Okay, let's all calm down," Miss Cheerilee announced, looking anything *but* calm. "Everypony take your seats, and we'll get to the bottom of this."

"Uh, Miss Cheerilee?" Snails motioned to the ceiling where all the seats in the classroom were currently stuck. Miss Cheerilee let out an exasperated sigh.

"Oh. Right. Okay, everypony just sit in the middle of the classroom and don't touch anything. I'm going to run and find Starlight Glimmer or Zecora or... somepony who can deal with...all this." As soon as Miss Cheerilee was gone, the ponies gathered in the center of the room and tried guessing what could have possibly happened.

"You think this is some kinda prank?" asked Silver Spoon.

"Well, if it ith, who did it?" demanded Twist.

"Forget who," said Scootaloo. "*How* did they do it?"

"Well, it *must* be a Unicorn." Diamond Tiara motioned to the desks and chairs above them. "This is *obviously* magic."

"That's a whole lotta magic for just a

prank!" said Snips. "I don't think *any* of us could do that. Could we?"

Apple Bloom glanced over her shoulder at Lilymoon, who was hanging back and not contributing to the conversation. Based on some of the looks the other ponies shot in Lilymoon's direction, Apple Bloom could tell she wasn't the only one who'd noticed. Pip wandered around the room examining the stacks of books.

"Well, whoever did it definitely took his or her time," Pip observed. "This must have taken all night!" Pip brushed too close to one of the stacks. It wobbled back and forth. "Oh bother," he muttered. Everypony gasped as the entire stack slowly teetered over and crashed onto the floor, sending books everywhere. The students looked around, but the other stacks remained standing, and the desks and chairs remained firmly on the ceiling. "Well, that wasn't too bad," Pip said, relieved.

One of the toppled books suddenly flew into the air. Diamond Tiara yelped. A second book flew up and slammed against the wall. Another book flew in the opposite direction, causing several ponies to duck. Something bumped Twist, knocking her backward. It was almost as if some invisible force were moving through the room, throwing books. Whatever it was, it was moving steadily in one direction.

It was moving right toward Pip!

CHAPTER FIVE

Pip backed away as the books flew into the
air in a path that led toward him. He zigged
and zagged out of the way, but no matter
where he moved, the invisible force changed
direction and continued toward him.

"Keep it away from me!" yelled Pip.
Scootaloo rushed toward the books flying
into the air but looked around, unsure
what to do next.

"Keep *what* away? There's nothing
here!" she exclaimed. The books stopped.
Nopony moved a muscle.

Suddenly, Pip launched up toward the
ceiling as if something had grabbed him
by the hoof. He shouted in alarm as the
classroom broke into pandemonium.

"What's happening?!" screamed Snips.

"Run for your lives!" yelled Snails.

"Somepony get me down from here!" Pip squealed as he flew through the air, weaving among the chairs and desks.

Apple Bloom searched the room for Lilymoon. She was standing out of the way in the corner, watching Pip intently. She took a step forward, as if she were about to do something.

But Sweetie Belle jumped in front of Apple Bloom, blocking her view. "We need to get him down from there!"

Apple Bloom watched Pip and got an idea. She turned to the others.

"Crusaders! Remember when we performed in the opening ceremonies of the Equestria Games?"

"Oh yeah!" Scootaloo said, grinning.

"I'm on it!" She ran to the back of the class to give herself some room. Sweetie Belle and Apple Bloom stood facing each other, their hooves outstretched between them. Scootaloo galloped toward her friends.

"One," counted Apple Bloom as Scootaloo leaped toward them.

"Two," Sweetie Belle continued as Scootaloo landed in her friends' hooves.

"*Three!*" Apple Bloom and Sweetie Belle said together as they hurled Scootaloo into the air.

Scootaloo flew through the classroom and slammed into Pip. Whatever had a hold of him let go, and they both flew into a pile of books, knocking the tower to the ground as they landed. Pip was a bit shaken up but otherwise unharmed.

Everypony rushed out of the Schoolhouse toward the playground and waited, silent and scared. But whatever had grabbed Pip seemed to have disappeared...for the moment, at least.

"Thith definitely theemth like more than jutht a prank," observed Twist.

"Well, if nopony else is going to point out the obvious, I will," Silver Spoon announced. "Nothing like this has ever happened before, so what's the big difference now?"

Silver Spoon turned and glared at Lilymoon, who was standing away from the other ponies. "Would *you* like to tell us anything, *Lilymoon*?" The students all glared at Lilymoon, waiting for her to respond to the accusation. She glared back at them.

"I have nothing to say to any of you,"

Lilymoon said defensively. Apple Bloom stepped forward.

"Now, everypony, just take a breath," Apple Bloom began. "Lilymoon, nopony is sayin' this is your fault or nothin'—"

"I think that's exactly what we're saying," Diamond Tiara interrupted. "You don't think it's a little bit odd that Lilymoon shows up, and the next thing you know, all *this* happens?"

"I ain't sayin' it's not odd," Apple Bloom said, "but this ain't the first crazy thing to ever happen in Ponyville. For all we know she could be just as confused as we are." She turned. "Lilymoon?"

Lilymoon glared at Apple Bloom. Instead of answering, she ran off.

Silver Spoon turned to Apple Bloom. "Looks pretty guilty to me."

CHAPTER SIX

Once Miss Cheerilee returned and heard what had happened to Pip, she announced that class was canceled and the Schoolhouse would be closed until they figured out just what was going on.

With the rest of the day free, the Cutie Mark Crusaders decided to head back to Sweet Apple Acres. Granny Smith was on a zap apple baking rampage, and the kitchen was bursting with baked goods. Apple Bloom knew there would be plenty to snack on while they discussed what to do about Lilymoon and the Schoolhouse. Apple Bloom, Sweetie Belle, and Scootaloo entered the kitchen to find Granny in the midst of baking a batch of zap apple pies to go along with the jams, tarts, muffins, and fritters that already filled the kitchen.

"Now hurry up and fix those pipes! I got another batch to make up for Golden Delicious after this'n!" Granny called out.

"Eeyup!" Big Mac replied from under the sink as he tinkered with the plumbing. Applejack walked into the kitchen carrying another bushel of zap apples. She set them down and wiped sweat from her brow.

"Here ya go, Granny," Applejack said. "This should do ya for the next coupla batches." Applejack saw the Crusaders in the kitchen and glanced up at the clock. "Hold up. Why aren't y'all in school?" she asked suspiciously.

"Miss Cheerilee let us out early today,"

Apple Bloom mentioned casually as she gathered some zap apple fritters to take up to her room. But her sister wasn't gonna let her off that easily.

"And why would Cheerilee let y'all out early?" Applejack pressed. "What happened?"

"Well, nopony knows *exactly* what happened," Scootaloo offered up. Apple Bloom shot her a look, but Scootaloo rolled her eyes and continued. "Something messed up the Schoolhouse. The whole place was a disaster. And then whatever did it grabbed Pip and flew him around the room!"

"Say *what*, now?!" Applejack exclaimed as Granny Smith and Big Mac stopped what they were doing to listen.

"A few of the ponies in class think the

new student has something to do with all of it. But we don't know that for sure yet," Sweetie Belle added.

"It's that new family up on Horseshoe Hill!" Granny Smith said. "That house has been empty for more moons than I care to count. Somethin' strange about it."

"Eeyup," Big Mac agreed.

"What's strange?" Apple Bloom asked.

"Well, nopony knows for sure," Granny said, placing some pies on the windowsill to cool. "But there's a reason it's been empty for so long. The ponies who lived there before...somethin' wasn't right about them, if I recall."

"Oh, that's just a buncha old ponies' tales," Applejack scoffed. She turned back to the Crusaders. "You said somethin' grabbed Pip and spun him? That sounds dangerous. Maybe I should head over to the castle, round up the others, and we can—"

"No! It's fine!" Apple Bloom said, louder than she intended. Everypony stopped and looked at her.

"Well, it don't sound fine to me," Applejack insisted, "and it won't hurt for me to mention to Twilight—"

"Ponies in Equestria *somehow* managed to survive before you and your friends came along, y'know!" Apple Bloom blurted out.

Applejack stared at her sister in surprise.

"Well, of course I know that. I'm just worried about you is all."

"Of *course* you're worried about me!" Apple Bloom said, rolling her eyes. "You're the almighty Applejack, hero of Equestria!

And I'm just your little sister who can't
do anything on her own!" Apple Bloom
stormed out of the kitchen and slammed
the door, leaving a very confused Apple
family—and the zap apple fritters—
behind her.

CHAPTER SEVEN

Apple Bloom sat at a table inside Sugarcube Corner eating one of Mrs. Cake's cupcakes. It wasn't as good as anything Granny Smith was currently baking, but on the plus side, there was no annoying big sister here trying to do everything for her.

Apple Bloom heard the door open and knew without looking it was Scootaloo and Sweetie Belle. They both sat down at the table and waited a few minutes before saying anything.

"So"—Scootaloo finally broke the silence—"that was...interesting."

Apple Bloom was embarrassed. She hadn't planned on blowing up at her sister, especially in front of her friends. She knew

Applejack just wanted to help. But if her sister was gonna run around saving the day all the time, what did that leave for Apple Bloom to do?

"We got our cutie marks. We're not little fillies anymore," Apple Bloom explained. "When Applejack was my age, she had already defeated Nightmare Moon!"

"Actually," Scootaloo said, doing the math in her head, "I don't think they were *quite* this young when—"

"The point is," Apple Bloom interrupted, "helpin' other ponies find their cutie marks is nice and all, but..." She trailed off.

"But our sisters and their friends save Equestria every other day..." Sweetie Belle finished for her.

"Yeah," Apple Bloom agreed. "We got some big hooves to fill."

Scootaloo put her wing on Apple Bloom's shoulder. "Look, we get it. Sweetie Belle feels the same way being Rarity's sister, and everypony knows I wish I were half as awesome as Rainbow Dash. But comparing yourself to the most heroic ponies in Equestria, one of whom happens to be your sister, is a *lot* of pressure!"

"I know," Apple Bloom admitted, "but I guess I just figured this stuff with Lilymoon happened at *our* Schoolhouse. With a pony *our* age. I was hoping it was something we could handle ourselves."

Scootaloo and Sweetie Belle glanced at each other and nodded.

"Well then, let's handle it," Scootaloo said, grinning.

"Really?" Apple Bloom asked.

"I guess so," Sweetie Belle said a little

nervously. "I mean, if I'm gonna do something completely terrifying, I may as well do it with my two best friends, right?"

"We're the Cutie Mark Crusaders," Scootaloo said. "We've done everything together for as long as I can remember. So if you think figuring out what's going on with Lilymoon is our next big mission, then you can count on us!"

Apple Bloom hugged her friends. She really was the luckiest pony in the whole world.

"Well, let's go over what we know so far. Lilymoon's family is from Trotsylvania and they live up in that house on Horseshoe Hill. Granny said something was up with that place. Maybe we can start there?"

"*Or,*" Scootaloo said, slamming her hooves on the table, "we return to the scene of the crime!" She smiled triumphantly.

"The Schoolhouse?" Sweetie Belle asked.

"No! The Everfree Forest!" Scootaloo corrected.

"Technically, that's not the scene of the crime," Sweetie Belle said matter-of-factly. "That's just where we spotted her." While the two of them bickered, Apple Bloom glanced out the window.

"Ugh. You know what I mean!" Scootaloo rolled her eyes.

"I just don't know why it makes sense to—" Sweetie Belle began, but Apple Bloom interrupted her.

"Scootaloo, you're a genius!" Apple Bloom announced.

"I am?" Scootaloo asked. Apple Bloom pointed. Sweetie Belle and Scootaloo looked out the window and, sure enough, there was Lilymoon, sneaking right back into the Everfree Forest!

CHAPTER EIGHT

"We can't just go rushing after her like we did last time," Apple Bloom said to the others as they hurried out of Sugarcube Corner.

"Well, what do you suggest? She's already got a head start," Scootaloo said impatiently.

Apple Bloom looked ahead. She could see Lilymoon was headed toward the same tree with the same big roots she had climbed over yesterday. If they just rushed after her, they would probably lose her again. Apple Bloom examined the options. She saw a larger entrance nearby with a clearer path.

"There!" Apple Bloom pointed. "We

can enter the Forest through there so we don't have to go crawling through the trees and bushes. It will let us get a little bit ahead, and then we can wait for her!" The other two nodded, and they veered toward the entrance.

"And we're *sure* this is how we want to spend our afternoon?" Sweetie Belle asked one more time.

"Yes!" Apple Bloom insisted.

They entered the Forest and ran as quickly as they could down the path. Once she thought they were far enough ahead, Apple Bloom motioned for the other two to slow down. They stopped and listened. Sure enough, in addition to the usual spooky sounds of the Forest, they could hear somepony walking through bushes and making just enough noise to be heard.

"This way, y'all," Apple Bloom whispered as she stepped off the path and picked her way carefully through the overgrown Forest. After all, it wouldn't do them any good if Lilymoon heard them coming.

As they got farther away from the path, Apple Bloom quickly realized that, as many times as the Crusaders had been in the Everfree Forest (and they had been in there more often than most), they had *never* been in this particular part before. Apple Bloom recalled Zecora had once mentioned that the Forest was much bigger than most ponies realized, even ponies who thought they understood the Everfree Forest. Apple Bloom was beginning to appreciate just how little she actually knew about it. Something about this part of the

Forest seemed wilder, more dangerous than the parts she knew (and those parts were no trot in the park!).

Up ahead, she saw what looked like a clearing and heard what she hoped was Lilymoon. She motioned to Scootaloo and Sweetie Belle, and the three of them crept up to a large tree with vines hanging from its branches. They brushed the vines to the side and peered slowly around the tree.

Lilymoon stood in the clearing. She was using her horn to levitate large rocks and stack them on top of one another.

"Look!" whispered Sweetie Belle. "It's *just* like the books in the Schoolhouse!"

"She *was* the one doing it," replied Scootaloo.

"But why's she doin' it out here?" whispered Apple Bloom.

Lilymoon continued stacking rocks and glancing around the Forest, as if she were expecting somepony to show up.

Apple Bloom took a step forward to get a closer look and stepped on a twig. It was small and made the tiniest snap, but it was enough to get Lilymoon's attention. She turned toward the Crusaders and stared at Apple Bloom, surprised.

"Lilymoon, we got a couple of questions for you," Apple Bloom said sternly as she stepped toward her. "Right, y'all?"

"*Mmpph mph MMMMPH*," she heard behind her. Apple Bloom turned.

Sweetie Belle and Scootaloo were wrapped up in vines. Their mouths were covered and they were being pulled slowly up into the branches of the tree!

CHAPTER NINE

"Lilymoon! *Stop it!*" Apple Bloom yelled, but when she turned, Lilymoon was gone! In a panic, Apple Bloom rushed toward the tree. She jumped up to grab her friends, but they were already too high to reach. She wasn't sure what to do! She looked around frantically, but there was nothing nearby she could use to reach them. So instead, she did what any Apple family member in her position would do. She started bucking the tree. Hard.

"Put!" **Buck.** *"My!"* **Buck.** *"Friends!"* **Buck.** *"Down!"* **Buck.** Surprisingly, this actually had an effect. The vines around

Sweetie Belle and Scootaloo loosened enough for them to get their mouths free.

"It's working!" Scootaloo yelled. "Keep hitting it!" Apple Bloom reared back her hooves when she felt something down near the ground. She looked and saw more vines wrapping themselves around her. The vines tugged and, with a scream, Apple Bloom was pulled up into the air to join the others.

"This is really bad." Sweetie Belle groaned.

"It's not *that* bad," said Apple Bloom as she tried unsuccessfully to grab on to a branch to stop her steady ascent.

"Not that bad?!" Sweetie Belle exclaimed. "A giant tree is pulling us to our doom and nopony even knows we're out here! How could it get any worse?!"

A noise caught the Crusaders' attention and they all turned to see Lilymoon standing nearby, watching the tree pull them higher and higher.

"Well," said Scootaloo, *"somepony* knows where we are." She glared down at Lilymoon. "So this is your plan? We catch you doing...whatever it is you're doing out here, so you have this tree attack us? We're the Cutie Mark Crusaders! We're gonna get out of this easily!" Scootaloo struggled harder, but the vines around them tightened.

Lilymoon didn't say anything. Instead, she rushed over to the trunk of the tree and started feeling around with her hooves. Whatever she was doing caused the tree to pull up the vines faster, as if it was in a hurry to do whatever it planned to do to the ponies.

"Lilymoon, *please!*" shouted Apple Bloom. "You don't have to do this!" Lilymoon ignored Apple Bloom as she continued searching around with her hooves. She reached underneath a lower branch and the entire tree shuddered. She pressed harder and the tree began to sway back and forth. The Crusaders all screamed as they rocked along with the tree. Lilymoon looked up one last time before rushing off into the Forest.

"*Great!*" Scootaloo yelled. "She sics her tree on us and takes off! What now?"

"*Help us! Anypony!*" Sweetie Belle yelled. Scootaloo and Apple Bloom joined in.

"*We're being eaten by a tree!*" Scootaloo yelled.

The tree continued swaying. As it did, the vines around the ponies loosened. They quickly became loose enough for the ponies to untangle themselves. Apple Bloom, Scootaloo, and Sweetie Belle jumped down and ran a safe distance away before turning back to watch the swaying tree. As they did, the tree slowed its back-and-forth motion until it eventually once again stood still. The vines dropped and hung innocently, but the Crusaders now knew better than to approach it.

"Why did it let us go?" Sweetie Belle asked.

"I bet our yelling scared it," Scootaloo said confidently.

"Seriously?" Sweetie Belle asked. "I don't think three ponies scared out of their minds screaming for help stopped the hungry tree."

"Lilymoon left," Apple Bloom said,

looking in the direction she ran. "As soon as she was gone, the tree stopped attacking us. She was doing it."

"Yeah! Because we know she's the one who messed up the Schoolhouse and attacked Pip!" Scootaloo said angrily.

"Should we go tell somepony? Like, maybe our sisters?" Sweetie Belle asked.

"No," Apple Bloom insisted. "We're goin' to Lilymoon's house on Horseshoe Hill and we are gonna get to the bottom of this."

"I knew that's what you were gonna say," Sweetie Belle said with a heavy sigh.

CHAPTER TEN

If Diamond Tiara hadn't told the Cutie
Mark Crusaders where the house on
Horseshoe Hill was, Apple Bloom was
sure they never would have found it. Now
that she was looking at it, she recognized
it was by far one of the largest houses in
Ponyville. But it was so tucked out of
the way that she had probably passed it
hundreds of times in her life and never
noticed it. Ponyville and the Everfree
Forest were right next to each other, but
there was usually a clear division where
one ended and the other began. High on
the hilltop, the house blended into the
Forest, almost like it was a part of it. Vines
wrapped around the walls of the five-story

cottage. Trees grew right next to it and branches brushed against the windows. The cottage itself seemed to be somehow wilder than other buildings in Ponyville.

"Wow," Scootaloo said, studying the house. "That is definitely the..."

"Scariest house in Ponyville?" Sweetie Belle finished. "Yeah, definitely the scariest house in Ponyville."

"It's *just* a house, y'all," Apple Bloom insisted. "Now, let's go get a better look." The ponies crept up the hill, careful to stay close to the trees and bushes so they wouldn't be spotted by anypony. They crept even closer to the house. The vines growing up against the wall wrapped tightly around the windows.

"Great," Sweetie Belle muttered, "more vines." Apple Bloom rolled her eyes and pushed the vines out of the way with her hoof. Through the window, they could see what looked like a workroom. There were jars filled with all kinds of things, strange plants lining the walls, lab equipment set out on tables, and two Unicorns—one male, one female—wearing goggles and standing next to a large cauldron. They had the same lavender complexion, blue mane, and piercing violet eyes as Lilymoon.

"Do you think those are Lilymoon's parents?" Scootaloo whispered. Apple Bloom shushed her and kept watching. One of the Unicorns, the male, poured vials filled with different liquids into the cauldron. The other Unicorn plucked leaves off a nearby plant and dropped them into the mixture as well. The cauldron bubbled violently as purple smoke poured out onto the floor.

"What kinda potion *is* that?" Apple Bloom wondered aloud. She squinted. It was getting harder to see what was going on; the window was so foggy.

"Uh. Apple Bloom?" Scootaloo tapped her with her hoof. Apple Bloom turned and realized it wasn't just the window getting foggy. A mist had come out of nowhere and surrounded them! Apple Bloom and the others tried to back away from the window, but their hooves stuck to the ground as if it were made of taffy.

"*Gross!*" Scootaloo yelled as her hooves sank into the ground.

"I can't move!" Sweetie Belle squeaked as she tried in vain to back away from the window. A chuckle echoed around them, but they couldn't see anypony through the fog.

"Wh-who's there?" Apple Bloom asked. "What do you want?"

"What do I want?" a crackly voice asked with another chuckle. "I'm not the one snooping into other ponies' business, now, am I?" A glowing horn appeared as the fog swirled away, revealing an old Unicorn. She was at least as old as Granny Smith (if not older) and had a tangled gray mess of a mane. She studied the Crusaders carefully. "Auntie Eclipse thinks you should answer your own question. What do *you* want?"

Before anypony could answer, an explosion from inside the house engulfed them all in smoke.

CHAPTER ELEVEN

In the commotion after the blast, Apple
Bloom realized she could move her
hooves again. She could hear Auntie
Eclipse coughing and didn't waste any
time. She turned to run in the opposite
direction.

"Run, y'all! This way!" she yelled.
Scootaloo and Sweetie Belle followed her,
leaving the old Unicorn behind them.

"I can't see anything!" Sweetie Belle
called.

"This way! Follow my voice!" Apple
Bloom shouted back. The purple fog was
beginning to clear up and Apple Bloom
could just make out the path they had taken
that would lead them back to Ponyville. But

before she could get there, another Unicorn jumped in her way, blocking them.

"Over here, Auntie!" she yelled. The fog had cleared enough for Apple Bloom to see the pony clearly. She was slightly older than the Crusaders and looked like Lilymoon but in reverse. A blue coat, a lavender tail, and a lavender mane with a single black streak running through it. She lowered her head and her horn glowed brightly, lifting the Crusaders off the ground.

"Hey! *Let us down!*" Scootaloo yelled. The Unicorn's horn glowed again and the Crusaders suddenly found they were unable to speak!

"Well done, Ambermoon!" Auntie Eclipse said as she walked slowly toward them. "Now we can get some answers!"

"Is everypony okay?" The female

Unicorn with the goggles came rushing out of the house. She saw Auntie Eclipse and the other Unicorn, Ambermoon, with the floating Crusaders. "What's going on out here?" she asked cautiously.

"Well, *that* didn't work," the male pony said as he walked outside. "We're *never* going to be able to break into the Livewood if we—"

"*Blue Moon!*" the female Unicorn said loudly, interrupting his thought mid-sentence. "We have intruders!" The male Unicorn, Blue Moon, raised his goggles and studied the Crusaders.

"Intruders? They're just—"

"Sticking their snouts where they don't belong!" Auntie Eclipse insisted. She turned to the Crusaders. "Now, who are you and what are you—"

"Auntie!" Ambermoon gasped. "Look!" Auntie Eclipse and the others followed Ambermoon's gaze. She was staring at the Crusaders' matching cutie marks.

"Well, look at that," Blue Moon whispered. He studied the Crusaders with renewed interest. "Who in Equestria are the three of you?"

"I know who they are," said a voice from the doorstep. Everypony turned to see Lilymoon standing there. "They go to my school. I'll deal with them."

"You didn't mention you were going to have guests," the female Unicorn with the goggles said.

"Sorry, Mother," Lilymoon said calmly, her eyes never leaving the Crusaders. "It must have slipped my mind." Lilymoon's mother nodded to Ambermoon. Her horn flashed as she released the Crusaders, dropping them gently to the ground. Lilymoon's mother looked down at them, her eyes darting to their cutie marks.

"I'm Lumi Nation, Lily's mother." She didn't smile as she spoke. In fact, she didn't seem particularly friendly at all. "This is her father, Blue Moon; her sister, Ambermoon; and our aunt Eclipse." Each of the Unicorns nodded to the Crusaders. "Lilymoon doesn't often bring friends around. We apologize for any confusion."

"No problem," Apple Bloom said, watching Lilymoon carefully as she spoke. "We just wanted to stop by and...see how you all were liking Ponyville so far."

"It's a little too nosy for my taste," Auntie Eclipse muttered. A look from Lumi Nation quieted her. Blue Moon grinned widely at the Crusaders, like he was trying a bit too hard to be friendly.

"Personally, I find Ponyville *full* of surprises," he said. "For example, I see you all have matching cutie marks. That's definitely...different." The entire family looked at the Crusaders expectantly.

"Yeah. It's actually pretty awesome." Scootaloo showed off her cutie mark. "Ponies are always interested, since we've got the only matching cutie marks in Equestria."

"I wouldn't be so sure about that," Auntie Eclipse whispered. Apple Bloom looked more closely at Lilymoon's family's cutie marks. Where Lilymoon had her spell book, Ambermoon had a potion bottle, Lumi Nation had a leaf, and Blue Moon had a star. But on top of those symbols, they each had the exact same bright moon, smoke, and lightning. Lilymoon's family had matching cutie marks, *just* like the Cutie Mark Crusaders!

CHAPTER TWELVE

Despite Lilymoon's family wanting to know absolutely *everything* about the CMCs and their matching cutie marks, Lilymoon convinced them she needed to talk to her "friends" alone. She brought the Crusaders into Auntie Eclipse's library. There were some old and dusty chairs, tables, and couches scattered throughout the room. A large map of Equestria hung on one wall. Below it was an equally large map of what looked like the Everfree Forest. There were strange artifacts lying around, and of course, most of the room was filled ceiling to floor with shelves of ancient-looking books. Lilymoon slid the library door closed and turned to glare at the Crusaders.

"What are you doing here?" she asked.

"We'll ask the questions!" Scootaloo said aggressively. "We saw what you were doing with those rocks in the Forest! *Just* like the books in the Schoolhouse! We caught you red-hooved! Don't try to deny it!"

"You don't know what you're talking about," Lilymoon responded flatly.

"Oh yeah? Then why did you have your tree attack us?" Scootaloo demanded.

Lilymoon snorted and rolled her eyes. "I saved the three of you from that Poison Joke Tree because you obviously have *no* idea how to take care of yourselves in the Forest."

"Poison Joke Tree? I thought Poison Joke was on the ground," Sweetie Belle said.

Apple Bloom wasn't sure what to think.

Lilymoon sighed. "Poison Joke *also* grows on trees. It's rare. But it happens. The vines pull you up until the leaves infect you. The only way to get free is to find the tree's ticklish spot."

"You were *tickling* the tree?!" Sweetie Belle asked incredulously. "You saved us?"

"Of course I did." Lilymoon arched an eyebrow. "I wasn't going to let you get hurt just because you were spying on me."

"We were spying on you because of what you did in the Schoolhouse!" Apple Bloom shot back.

"I wasn't the one who did that to the Schoolhouse!" Lilymoon said angrily. But then her face fell and she looked away.

"But I *am* still the one who's responsible," she added quietly.

"Say what, now?" Apple Bloom asked.

Lilymoon studied the Crusaders as if she was weighing her options. "It was a bogle," she finally said.

"What's a bogle?" asked Scootaloo.

"A bogle is a creature that lives deep in forests. They're very rare. Just like Poison Joke Trees." Lilymoon's cold exterior melted *slightly* as she explained things.

"Are they scary-looking?" asked Sweetie Belle.

"Nopony knows exactly what they look like. They're invisible," Lilymoon explained. "In fact, there's a *lot* ponies don't know about them." She walked over to one of the bookshelves and searched. "That's why my family moved here," she added.

"For bogles?" asked Apple Bloom.

"No," Lilymoon said as she searched, "to be closer to the Everfree Forest. It's kind of an obsession, to be honest. There's just so much ponies don't know about it. Here!" She used her horn to levitate a book off the shelf, placing it on a nearby table.

"*The Lost Creatures of Equestria*," she read as she blew dust off the cover. "This book contains the only recorded mention of bogles." Lilymoon flipped through the book until she came to the page she was looking for.

"'Bogles tend to keep to themselves,'" she read. "'They're very territorial and mark their nests with elaborate decoration. Methods can include but are not limited to: scratching symbols in trees, bright colors, stacking and levitation of objects—basically anything that makes their nest look as unique as possible. They get furious if anything disturbs their home.'" Lilymoon looked down at her hooves. "I wanted to observe a bogle in its natural habitat. I found the nest when I went into the Forest after school, but the bogle wasn't there. I went back and checked again this morning. I didn't think it was there. I should have been more careful.... I knocked over a couple of rocks...."

She sighed and then continued reading. "'Once provoked, the bogle abandons its nest and tracks the creature who disturbed it. It builds a new nest in the victim's home. If it likes its new surroundings more than its old nest, it's almost impossible to force it to leave.'" Lilymoon looked at the Crusaders. "I got to the Schoolhouse early.

So did the bogle. I think it *really* likes the Schoolhouse."

"Wow. So this really *was* all your fault!" Scootaloo blurted out. Lilymoon looked away, embarrassed.

"Okay, okay," Apple Bloom said. "No use cryin' over spilled cider. How do we get rid of it?"

"That's the problem," Lilymoon said, flipping to the next page. "It doesn't say anything else about bogles. I was hoping when class started, all the noise would scare it off. But that obviously didn't happen. So I tried rebuilding its old nest, hoping it would miss it and return. But I don't think it wants to leave the Schoolhouse." She looked at the Crusaders, and for the first time she wasn't glaring at them. She seemed scared. "I don't think there *is* a way to get rid of it!"

CHAPTER THIRTEEN

"There has to be *some* way to get rid of it!" Scootaloo insisted. "This is your aunt's library, right? Maybe we could ask her?"

"No!" Lilymoon said firmly. "We can't do that!"

"Why not?" Sweetie Belle asked.

"Because." Lilymoon glanced back, making sure the door to the foyer was still closed. "I'm not supposed to go out into the Forest without them."

"So what were you doin' out there?" Apple Bloom asked. Lilymoon sat down in one of the ancient chairs, and a cloud of dust flew around her.

"My father is an expert on reading the stars. Astrology, science, magic. My mother spent her life studying the plants of Equestria. She can recognize every leaf, root, branch, and berry that exists, especially the ones with magical properties. My sister is a natural with potions and spells, and Auntie Eclipse...well...she knows everything about anything that has ever happened in Equestria."

"They sound smart! Why don't we want to ask them how to get rid of the bogle again?" Sweetie Belle asked, confused.

"I can hear exactly what they would say." Lilymoon groaned. *"Oh, Lilymoon, you shouldn't have gone out alone. Oh, Lilymoon, don't mess with things you don't understand. Oh, Lilymoon, why can't you be brilliant and amazing just like the rest of us? Oh, Lilymoon, why are you such a disappointment?"* Lilymoon frowned at the Crusaders. "My family has very high expectations. I was exploring the forests of Trotsylvania with my mother when I got my cutie mark. We were studying the flight patterns of perytons."

"What's a peryton?" asked Scootaloo.

"Not now!" scolded Apple Bloom. She nodded to Lilymoon to continue.

"I wasn't sure what a book had to do with magical creatures. I thought maybe I was supposed to study and catalog them. That's why I was trying to study the bogle. I don't know. I just want to show my family I'm good at something. You all wouldn't understand."

"Actually," Apple Bloom said, "I think we have a pretty good idea of what it's like to want to figure out what you're good at and prove yourself to ponies you look up to."

"You do?" Lilymoon asked.

"Definitely." Apple Bloom turned to the others. "So, Crusaders? What do ya say?"

"I say we're gonna come up with a plan to catch a bogle," Scootaloo said.

"I say I'm gonna regret everything about this," Sweetie Belle said with a groan.

Lilymoon stared at the Crusaders. She looked confused. "Why would you help me?" she asked.

"That's what friends do," Apple Bloom responded simply.

"I don't have friends," Lilymoon replied.

"Well, with that attitude, I can see why," Scootaloo fired back. Apple Bloom shot her a look. "What?" Scootaloo asked innocently.

"She's right," Lilymoon admitted. "I don't know if you noticed, but my family isn't exactly 'warm and fuzzy.' I guess I've always come across a little different. So nopony ever asked to be my friend and I never tried."

"Well, you got three friends now," Apple Bloom said. "And we're gonna help you fix this."

"Thank you," Lilymoon said, relief flooding her face.

"Now," Apple Bloom said, "let's think this through." She paced back and forth. "You said bogles like decorating their nests, right?" Lilymoon nodded. "And they *hate* when anypony disturbs them?"

"Pip found that out the hard way," Scootaloo reminded them.

"Well then, the first part of the plan is easy. We mess up the Schoolhouse and make the bogle mad," Apple Bloom said to the others.

"That is a *terrible* plan." Sweetie Belle groaned. "I don't know about you ponies, but I would prefer *not* to be grabbed by my hooves and tossed around the room by an invisible monster."

"He would have to catch us first," Scootaloo said confidently.

"That could work," Lilymoon said, "but *then* what? It didn't leave the Schoolhouse last time. I think it likes it too much in there!"

"Yeah, but if we had somewhere better we could lead it…" Scootaloo thought aloud.

"It's gonna have to be *reallllly* nice to convince it to leave," Lilymoon pointed out.

"Well, no offense, but your rock stacks weren't all that impressive," Scootaloo responded. They all sat and thought about it.

"Maybe the bogle is just tired of living in the woods?" Sweetie Belle suggested.

"How does that help us?" Scootaloo asked, rolling her eyes. "Unless you wanna let it live with you and Rarity?"

"No way!" Sweetie Belle squeaked. "Rarity loves her boutique. And she's scary when you mess with her stuff."

"Wait a minute!" Apple Bloom exclaimed. "I bet the bogle would love Rarity's stuff, too! It's way prettier than rocks and sticks in the woods!"

"What? No!" Sweetie Belle squealed nervously. "We are *not* setting a bogle loose in my sister's shop!"

"Of course not," Apple Bloom said. "But we *are* gonna need to borrow some of her stuff. Here's what we're gonna do..."

CHAPTER FOURTEEN

The Ponyville Schoolhouse, which was so welcoming during the day, looked incredibly creepy at night. *Of course*, thought Apple Bloom, *that might be because we know there is an invisible monster lurking inside.* The ponies hid in the bushes by the playground and looked warily at the school.

"Everything is set up. This is it. Is everypony ready?" Apple Bloom asked.

"*Why* are we doing this at night, again?" Sweetie Belle replied nervously.

"For the *hundredth* time, we are doing it at night because we don't want an invisible bogle knocking over every single pony in Ponyville during the day!" Scootaloo said.

"Okay, okay," Sweetie Belle muttered. "Doesn't make it any less scary!"

"We have the paint?" Apple Bloom asked.

"Yes." Lilymoon nodded toward the bag next to her.

"I just hope Rarity doesn't notice everything we borrowed," Sweetie Belle said.

"It's for a good cause," Apple Bloom reminded her. The ponies all sat in the bushes, none of them moving.

"Maybe we should go check everything in the Forest one more time?" Sweetie Belle suggested.

"No more stallin'. It's time to get in there," Apple Bloom said. "Let's go." The ponies all crawled out of the bushes and approached the Schoolhouse. They crept up the steps toward the front door. It was chained shut with a giant padlock on it.

"Oh well. Guess that's that," Sweetie Belle said, turning to walk down the steps. Scootaloo stopped her while Apple Bloom and Lilymoon studied the lock.

"Think you can pick it?" Apple Bloom asked.

"I don't know how to pick a lock!" Lilymoon said, annoyed.

"Hey, guys!" Scootaloo whispered.

"Can't you use magic?" Apple Bloom whispered.

"Guys!" Scootaloo said louder.

"I don't know that kind of magic," Lilymoon insisted.

"*Guys!*" Scootaloo called. Apple Bloom and Lilymoon turned. Scootaloo and

Sweetie Belle were standing next to one of the Schoolhouse windows. Scootaloo slid it open. "Not *every*thing needs to be super complicated. Come on!" Apple Bloom and Lilymoon hurried down the stairs with the bag of supplies and followed Scootaloo and Sweetie Belle through the window and into the Schoolhouse.

The Schoolhouse was dark. Even with Lilymoon and Sweetie Belle lighting their horns, it was still hard to see. The books were all restacked in precarious arches, each book carefully placed. The desks and chairs had been removed from the ceiling and now magically lined the sides of the walls. In their place, pictures drawn by the students plastered the ceiling in strange patterns. Miss Cheerilee's desk was in the center of the Schoolhouse, upside down on the floor. The curtains from the windows were placed in swirling shapes around it. Apple Bloom's ears perked up.

"*Shhhh.* Y'all hear that?" she asked. The ponies listened quietly. Steady breathing was coming from the center of the room.

"Is the bogle snoring?" Scootaloo asked. Apple Bloom nodded. She motioned to the bag next to Scootaloo.

"Get ready," Apple Bloom whispered. Scootaloo reached in and pulled out two cans of paint. She handed one to Lilymoon and held on to the other one.

"Ready," Scootaloo whispered back. Apple Bloom nodded to Sweetie Belle, who nervously rushed over to one side of the classroom while Apple Bloom headed to the other side. Scootaloo and Lilymoon quietly carried the cans of paint as close as they dared to Miss Cheerilee's desk. Everypony turned to watch Apple Bloom for the signal. Apple Bloom gulped and quickly wondered if Applejack was ever this scared when she was saving Equestria. She pushed the thought aside and looked to make sure everypony was ready.

"Now!" Apple Bloom yelled. She kicked hard, knocking over the stack of books closest to her. Sweetie Belle leaped onto one of the chairs stuck to the wall and pried it down. It fell to the ground with a loud crash. The snoring in the center of the room stopped. Scootaloo and Lilymoon both heaved the paint cans. Pink and

purple paint flew through the room and landed on...something.

That very scary *something* covered in pink and purple paint rose slowly and let out a ferocious roar. The bogle was awake.

CHAPTER FIFTEEN

"I think we made it mad!" Scootaloo
yelled as she kicked over another pile of
books.

"Ya think?!" Apple Bloom called back.
"Keep it up! We need to make sure it's
really, really mad!" The ponies rushed
around the room, destroying as much as
they could while avoiding the angry bogle.
Apple Bloom couldn't make out all the
details (the bogle was still invisible), but
thanks to the pink and purple paint, she
could see it was a little bit smaller than
Big Mac and had horns on top of its head;
massive arms; long, spindly legs; and a
powerful spiked tail. No wonder it was
invisible. It was ugly!

"Okay, the first part of the plan worked!" Sweetie Belle squealed as the bogle rushed toward her. It tried to grab her, but she ran between its legs. "Can we get to the second part now? *Please?!*"

"Everypony out the window!" Apple Bloom yelled. The ponies all rushed toward the front of the Schoolhouse. They dived through the open window and landed in a heap in the bushes below.

"It's coming!" Lilymoon grunted. The ponies untangled themselves and ran across the playground. Apple Bloom looked back over her shoulder just in time to see the bogle crash through the front door of the Schoolhouse, easily breaking the chain and lock.

"Miss Cheerilee is *not* gonna like that!" Sweetie Belle wailed.

"At least the monster isn't *in* the Schoolhouse anymore!" Scootaloo said. "That's progress!" They ran toward the bushes, and Scootaloo brushed some leaves and branches aside, revealing her scooter.

"Okay, Scootaloo, you go ahead and make sure everything's ready," Apple Bloom ordered. "We'll be right behind you!"

Scootaloo nodded as she put on a headlamp and jumped onto her scooter. She sped off into the darkness.

Apple Bloom turned to see the bogle knock aside the playground's seesaw as it rushed toward them. She nodded at the others and they took off in the same direction as Scootaloo, the bogle close behind them.

They rushed through the empty streets of Ponyville, always turning back to make sure the bogle was following. Apple Bloom looked ahead and could see the edge of the Everfree Forest and the path the Crusaders had used earlier to follow Lilymoon. She couldn't believe that had been just this afternoon! When she woke up this morning she never would have guessed she would end the day being chased through the center of town by an invisible monster.

"Come on, y'all! The Forest is just over there!" Apple Bloom called. They rushed toward the path. Behind them, the bogle knocked over carts and took chunks out of several buildings as it rushed to catch them.

Apple Bloom hoped her plan would work. She didn't want to find out what the bogle was going to do to them if they failed.

CHAPTER SIXTEEN

Apple Bloom ran as fast as she could next to Lilymoon and Sweetie Belle, their horns the only source of light now that the moon and stars were blocked by the leafy canopy of the Everfree Forest.

"You sure this is the right way?" Lilymoon asked Apple Bloom.

"I think so?" Apple Bloom said, squinting into the darkness.

"Look! Over there!" Sweetie Belle shouted. Apple Bloom saw a bright light ahead of them. She and the others rushed toward it.

The ponies raced into the clearing where Lilymoon had originally found the bogle. Only now, it was completely transformed!

It didn't look anything like it had earlier in the day. Lanterns hung from tree branches, bathing the clearing in a warm, cozy glow. Fabrics of every color and pattern were stretched between the trees, creating a colorful tapestry that flowed gently in the breeze. Rocks were arranged carefully in swirling patterns on the ground, and in the center of all of it, piles of cloth were organized into an inviting nest.

"Psssssst!" A voice from above caught Apple Bloom's attention. She looked up to see Scootaloo waving to them from the branches of a tree. Apple Bloom, Sweetie Belle, and Lilymoon rushed up to join her. They all quietly watched the clearing below.

The paint-covered bogle burst into the clearing, expecting to find a bunch of scared ponies. Instead, it found its transformed nest. It stopped, looking around, confused. It growled menacingly as it slowly circled the clearing. It brushed its tail along the cloth and gently tapped the lanterns, watching them sway back and forth. It studied the patterns of the rocks on the ground, tapping each one with a claw as it passed.

"I think it's working," Scootaloo whispered.

"*Shhhhh!* Quiet!" Sweetie Belle hissed.

The bogle tested the nest of fabrics in the center of the clearing. It sniffed them, rearranged them, sniffed them again, and finally plopped down and burrowed into them.

"I think the bogle likes its old nest again," Lilymoon said.

"Well, as my sister would say, you can't

argue with good taste," Sweetie Belle added. Below them, the bogle purred happily. Rocks floated magically into the air as the bogle rearranged them into new patterns.

"*Awww.* It's kinda cute when it's not roaring and chasing you," Scootaloo said, grinning.

"Uh. *One* question," Sweetie Belle whispered to the others. "Now that the bogle is happy...how are we getting out of this tree?" The ponies all looked at one another.

"I guess we gotta wait for it to go back to sleep?" Apple Bloom said.

"That's what I was afraid you were gonna say," Sweetie Belle said, yawning. She and the others settled in as comfortably as they could to wait for the bogle to go to bed.

CHAPTER SEVENTEEN

Apple Bloom didn't remember falling asleep. But she must have, because the next thing she could remember was waking up to Sweetie Belle gently nudging her with her hoof.

"I think it's safe," Sweetie Belle whispered. Apple Bloom peered sleepily down at the bogle's nest. Some of Rarity's fabric was magically hovering in the air over the bogle's nest. It was curled up underneath them, still covered in paint, and snoring loudly.

"Those lanterns are brighter than they were before," Apple Bloom said with another yawn.

"That's not the lanterns," Scootaloo

said. Apple Bloom blinked a few times and realized the warm glow wasn't coming from the lanterns but instead from the sky in the east.

"Oh Celestia! We've been out all night!" Apple Bloom yelped loudly enough that the bogle below snorted and stirred. The ponies all froze until it resumed its snoring. Apple Bloom and the others carefully crawled out of the tree and slowly snuck around the edge of the bogle's nest, careful not to disturb anything. Once they were a good distance away, Sweetie Belle turned to the others.

"Do you think that's it?" she asked. "It's just gonna stay there?"

"I *think* so," Lilymoon said slowly. "Everything I read made it sound like if a bogle loves its nest, it just wants to be left alone. I think as long as nopony goes looking for it again, we should be fine."

"Let's hope so," Apple Bloom said as they walked out of the Everfree Forest into Ponyville.

"Uh-oh," Scootaloo said. The Crusaders and Lilymoon watched as ponies rushed around, shouting and examining the destruction left by the bogle. Scootaloo turned to the others. "You think we're gonna get in trouble for this?"

"There you are!" a voice called from up ahead. Apple Bloom saw Applejack marching toward her, Granny Smith and Big Mac close behind.

"Eeyup," Apple Bloom said.

"We've been worried *sick*! Where in the name of Celestia have y'all been all night?" Applejack shouted as she marched toward the Crusaders. Before Apple Bloom could answer, another voice broke through the crowd.

"Lilymoon! What have you done?" Lumi Nation shouted as she and Blue Moon came bursting through the crowd.

"Hey, y'all…" Apple Bloom said. "So, what happened was—"

"I went into the Everfree Forest by myself and a bogle followed me out," Lilymoon admitted, stepping in front of Apple Bloom. "That's what attacked the school. I'm to blame. The Cutie Mark Crusaders helped me lure it back into the Forest where it wouldn't hurt anypony." Lilymoon turned to Apple Bloom. "I couldn't have done it without…my friends." Lilymoon's parents' eyes went wide.

"A bogle?" her father asked. "Really?"

"Tell us everything," her mother said. "How did you lure it? What did it look like? Oh, darling, I'm so impressed!"

"Impressed?!" Granny Smith blurted out. "I'd be more impressed if she'd leave dangerous monsters alone in the first place." Lilymoon's parents glanced at the Apple family and shared a look.

"Yes. Well. We need to get Lilymoon home," Lumi Nation said curtly.

"We apologize for any problems this might have caused," Blue Moon said. "We will keep a closer eye on Lily. No need to bother her. Come, Lilymoon!" Her parents turned and walked off. Lilymoon obediently followed but looked back and mouthed the words *thank you* to the Crusaders as she walked away.

"Yeah," Scootaloo said, "there's definitely something strange about that family." Sweetie Belle and Apple Bloom nodded. Applejack looked down at Apple Bloom.

"Is what she said true?" Applejack asked. "You went and helped her catch this bogle thing she set loose?"

"Yeah," Apple Bloom replied.

"And why didn't you ask for my help?" Applejack looked more hurt than angry.

"Because..." Apple Bloom glanced at Scootaloo and Sweetie Belle, who nodded encouragingly. She turned to Applejack. "You're my big sister and I love you, but you save Equestria, like, every other day. I just wanted to show you I can be as brave as you are." Apple Bloom looked down sheepishly. Applejack studied her sister thoughtfully.

"Now listen," Applejack finally said. "You are one of the bravest ponies I've ever met in my life...and I know some pretty brave ponies. But you're also my little sister. I'm always gonna worry about you, and I'm always gonna want to help you. It don't mean I think you can't help yourself. It's just what big sisters do. Got it?"

"You really think I'm brave?" Apple Bloom asked, smiling.

"Of course I do!" Applejack replied. Apple Bloom considered that for a second.

"Well," she finally said, "then just stop bein' so amazing all the time, and I won't have to work so hard to keep up."

Applejack burst out laughing and hugged her sister tightly. "I'll get right to work on that. But listen up." She looked at Scootaloo and Sweetie Belle, including them in what she said. "One thing my friends and I never do is run and go *lookin'* for danger. I have a feelin' y'all are gonna have plenty of adventures that are gonna give us all kinds of panic attacks. But don't go makin' trouble when you don't need to. Y'all shoulda told us about this bogle."

"We're sorry," Sweetie Belle said.

"But we *were* pretty awesome," Scootaloo added.

"I have no doubt," Applejack said, grinning, "and if I'm bein' honest, I'm pretty impressed. Y'all are gonna have to tell me all about this bogle."

A shriek ripped through the morning air, causing everypony to freeze.

"What in Equestria happened to my fabrics?!" Rarity screamed from her boutique.

Sweetie Belle slowly turned to the others. "We are in *so* much trouble."

EPILOGUE

The Pony once again looked out the window at the expansive Everfree Forest. Not with excitement this time but with concern. The Pony opened the *Book of Legends* and flipped through the pages. Things The Pony had been certain of seemed less so now. There were questions where there hadn't been before. The events of the past couple of days had changed things drastically.

The Pony would have to be patient. Plans would have to wait. The bogle had caused too much attention. And then there was the issue of the three little ponies with the matching cutie marks. That required further investigation. That was unexpected. There was too much at stake here to leave anything to chance. If The Pony's plan was going to succeed, something would have to be done about the Cutie Mark Crusaders.

NOW ON DVD!

TWILIGHT AND STARLIGHT